Do-It-Yourself Science™

EXPERIMENTS
on the
WEATHER

Zella Williams

PowerKiDS press™

New York

Published in 2007 by The Rosen Publishing Group, Inc.
29 East 21st Street, New York, NY 10010

First Edition

Editor: Joanne Randolph
Book Design: Greg Tucker and Ginny Chu

Photo Credits: Cover © Trapdoor Media/Shutterstock; p. 5 © Royalty-Free/Artville; pp. 6, 7, 8, 9, 12, 13, 14, 15, 16, 17 by Cindy Reiman; pp. 10, 11 by Adriana Skura; pp. 18, 19 by Scott Bauer; pp. 20, 21 by Shalhevet Moshe; p. 22 Shutterstock.com.

Library of Congress Cataloging-in-Publication Data

Williams, Zella.
  Experiments on the weather / Zella Williams. — 1st ed.
      p. cm. — (Do-it-yourself science)
  Includes index.
  ISBN-13: 978-1-4042-3663-9 (library binding)
  ISBN-10: 1-4042-3663-5 (library binding)
  1. Weather—Experiments—Juvenile literature. I. Title.
  QC981.3.W54 2007
  551.6078—dc22
                                    2006027569

Manufactured in the United States of America

Contents

What's the Weather? 4

Warming Up Earth 6

Fast Wind, Slow Wind 8

The Power of the Wind 10

Make Your Own Cloud 12

How Much Rain? 14

Under Pressure 16

Make a Thermometer 18

Weather Watcher 20

Weather Is Fun! 22

Glossary 23

Index 24

Web Sites 24

What's the Weather?

Some days it rains. Some days it is hot and sunny. Sometimes it is windy or cold. Weather is happening all the time. We pay attention to it so we know how to dress or so we can plan our day. Is it a day for the beach, or a day to curl up with a book inside?

Scientists who study the weather are called **meteorologists**. Try the **experiments** in this book so you can learn more about the weather, too.

These colorful flags let people know how windy it is.

Earth is circled by miles (km) of gases called the **atmosphere**. These gases make our weather possible. Without the atmosphere, Earth would be a very cold and windy place. The gases in the atmosphere let heat in to reach Earth but do not let it leave. This is called the **greenhouse effect**.

You will need

- two thermometers
- a zip-seal plastic bag big enough to fit one of the thermometers
- a sunny day

1 Place one of the **thermometers** in the plastic bag and seal it. A thermometer is a tool that tells how hot or cold something is.

2 On a sunny day, find a spot outside without shade. Put the thermometers next to each other in the sunny spot.

3 Wait 15 minutes.

4 Read the thermometers. Does one show a warmer **temperature** than the other? The thermometer that has been in the plastic bag should have a higher temperature than the one without a bag. The Sun's rays, which make heat, enter the bag and the heat cannot get out easily. This is also how the atmosphere works. It traps heat around Earth.

Fast Wind, Slow Wind

The air around Earth is always moving. Warm air rises, and cool air sinks. As the air moves around, it makes wind. Strong winds happen when really warm air meets really cool air. You can find out how fast the wind is moving by using a tool called an **anemometer**.

You will need

- five 6-ounce (177 ml) paper cups
- two drinking straws
- scissors, or a tool used to cut
- a large pin
- a pencil with an eraser
- a felt-tip pen
- tape
- a 26-ounce (769 ml) cup or bowl filled with clay or play dough.

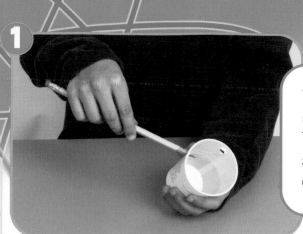

1 Take your pencil and poke four holes near the rim of one of your cups. There should be the same amount of space between each hole. Poke another hole in the bottom of the cup.

2 Slide each straw through two of the facing holes in the cup's rim so that the straws cross to form an X. One straw will cross above the other.

3

Tape the bottom of one cup to the end of one straw. Tape the other three cups to the other three ends of the straws. Make sure the cups all face in the same direction. Use a felt-tip pen to make a mark on one of the cups. The colored cup will make it easier to see how fast your anemometer moves in the wind.

4

Carefully push a pin through the center of your straw X. Poke your pencil through the hole in the bottom of the cup, eraser side up. Now push the pin into the eraser of the pencil, and stick the other end of the pencil into your cup of clay or play dough. You have made an anemometer! Place your anemometer outside. If it is very windy, the cups will spin quickly. If there is little wind, they will spin slowly.

The Power of the Wind

We use many of Earth's **resources** to make **electricity**. Some of these resources will someday be used up. Some resources, like the wind and the Sun, will not be used up. These resources can be caught and turned into electricity. Weather has power! Try this.

You will need

- an 8-by-8-inch (20 x 20 cm) piece of heavy paper or poster board
- a ruler
- a pencil
- a pair of scissors
- a thumbtack
- a wooden stick ¼ inch (6 mm) around and about 2 feet (61 cm) long

1 Use a ruler to draw an X on the piece of paper. Make your X by laying the ruler down so that it passes through the top right corner and the bottom left corner of the paper. Use the pencil to draw a line. Do the same for the other two corners.

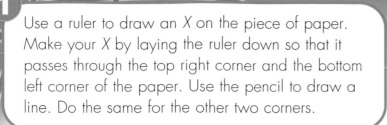

At the center of the X, draw a 1-by-1-inch (2.5 x 2.5 cm) square. The center of the X also should be the center of the square.

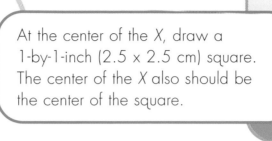

3

Starting at one corner, cut along the pencil line until you reach the square. Do the same for the other three corners. Be sure to stop cutting when you reach the square so the piece of paper stays together. You should have four triangles.

4

Bend the left corner of each triangle into the center, but do not press the paper to make a fold. Use a thumbtack to hold down the corners at the center and to fix the windmill to the wooden stick. Take your windmill outside on a windy day and watch it spin. The power from the wind turns the blades!

Make Your Own Cloud

Have you ever tried to see shapes in the clouds? Clouds are made when tiny drops of water in the air cool and stick together around bits of dust. These bits of water-covered dust gather together to form clouds. Try this to make your own cloud.

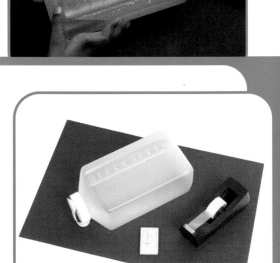

You will need

- a clean 2.12-quart (2 liter) soda or juice bottle
- a sheet of black paper
- clear tape
- hot water
- matches
- an adult to help

1

Tape the black paper to a wall near a flat place where you can set a bottle and see it easily. The paper will help you see your cloud better.

2

Have an adult help you dump about 1 cup (237 ml) of very hot water into a bottle. Blow into the bottle to make sure that it is as big as it can be, and put the top on. Shake the bottle for about 1 minute. This will put tiny bits of water into the air in the bottle.

3

Ask an adult to light a match. Let it burn for a few seconds, take off the bottle top, quickly put the match in the bottle, and put the top back on. The match should be burning when you drop it in the bottle, but it will go out when it hits the water. The smoke makes bits of dust in the air where the water can gather.

4

Lay the bottle on its side and push down on the side for about 10 seconds. Place the bottle in front of the black paper. Do you see a cloud? Push down until you see a cloud form.

The tiny water drops that make clouds can stay in the air as long as they are small and light. When the air cools, the drops begin to stick together. Soon they become too heavy to stay in the clouds. They fall to the ground as rain, snow, sleet, or **hail**. How much rain falls to the ground where you live?

You will need

- a tall 8-ounce (237 ml) cup on which you can write
- a ruler
- a marker that will not wash off
- paper and a felt-tip pen

1

Hold a ruler against the side of the cup. Make sure the bottom of the ruler lines up with the bottom of the cup.

2

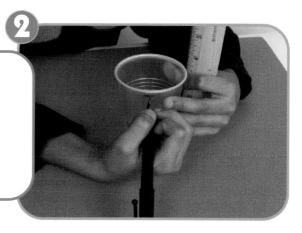

Use a permanent marker to draw lines that are 1 inch (2.5 cm) apart up to the top of the cup. You have made a rain gauge! A rain gauge is a tool that measures how much rain falls.

3

Place the rain gauge outside on something flat. After it rains go out and measure how much rain fell into your gauge. Record the date, time, and amount of rain.

4

After you have five or six measurements, make a chart of the different amounts of rain on different days. Do they change much? Wait a few months and try it again. Does your chart look different?

Under Pressure

The air has a weight that pushes down on us. We call this air **pressure**. Cold air is heavy and pushes down on us a lot. This is called high pressure. Warm air is light and pushes down on us less. It is called low pressure. Low pressure often means wet weather is coming. High pressure means dry, sunny days. You can make a **barometer** to measure air pressure.

You will need

- a 26-ounce (769 ml) wide-mouth jar
- a 3-by-5-inch (8 x 13 cm) card
- a balloon
- scissors
- tape
- a straw
- a rubber band
- a felt-tip pen

1

Cut a piece of rubber from a balloon that is big enough to fit over the mouth of the jar.

2

Pull the piece of balloon tightly over the mouth of the jar and fix the balloon to the jar with a rubber band. Make sure no air can get in the jar. Tape the straw to the top of the balloon.

3

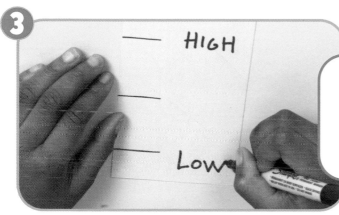

Draw three lines across the card about 1 inch (2.5 cm) apart. On the top line write "high," and on the bottom line write "low."

4

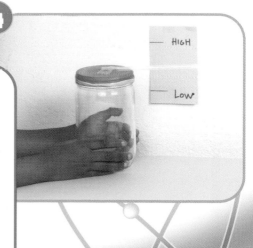

Place the jar on something flat in front of a wall indoors. Tape the card to the wall so that the middle mark lines up with the straw. Check the position of the straw once a day for a week and see if it moves. On cold days the straw should point toward the high-pressure line. On warm days the straw should point toward the low-pressure line. If you watch the straw carefully, it will help you guess when the weather is going to change.

Make a Thermometer

A thermometer is the tool we use to measure the temperature. We use it to find out how hot or cold our bodies are or the air outside is. A big part of tracking the weather is knowing the temperature outside. Let's make a thermometer for use outside.

You will need

- a clear, bendable tube 1 foot (30.5 cm) long and 2 inches (5 cm) across (available at hardware stores)
- two stoppers to fit the tube ends
- rubbing alcohol
- food coloring
- heavy string
- a metal hanger
- paper
- a marker that will not wash off in the rain
- rubber gloves and safety glasses or an adult to help
- a notebook and pen

1 Use a 1-foot (30.5 cm) **tube**. Tightly close one end of the tube with a stopper. This will be the bottom of the thermometer. Fill the tube halfway with rubbing alcohol. Wear safety gloves and glasses, or ask an adult for help.

2 Add a little red food coloring and put a stopper in the open end of the tube.

3 Fix a piece of paper with lines drawn 1 millimeter apart to a tree. Tie the thermometer to the tree in front of the piece of paper. You will use this to figure out the temperature.

4 Call a nearby office of the National Weather Service or check the radio for the current temperature. Mark the level of the alcohol in the tube on the paper behind your thermometer. Write down the temperature next to the mark. Do this each day for a week. You will now have a guide for which line the alcohol reaches at a given temperature. Have fun using your thermometer!

Weather Watcher

Do you like to go outside and play? What about when it is raining? Or when it is cloudy or very cold? The weather can really change what we do. You can guess what the weather will be by making **observations**. Making observations is a big part of being a scientist. Let's try an experiment.

You will need

- a notebook